JEASY 741.5973 HOW NO. 2
A Scooby-Doo! #2, A merry
scary holiday
Howard, Lee.

D1010855

SCOOBY-DOO! A MERRY SCARY HOLIDAY

Adapted by Lee Howard
Illustrated by Alcadia Scn
Based on the episode "A Scooby-Doo Christmas" by John Collier,
George Doty IV, Jim Krieg, and Ed Scharlach

No part of this publication may be reproduced in whole or in part, stored in a retrieval system, or transmitted in any form or by any means, electronic, mechanical, photocopying, recording, or otherwise, without written permission of the publisher. For information regarding permission, write to Scholastic Inc., Attention: Permissions Department, 557 Broadway, New York, NY 10012.

ISBN 978-0-545-36865-0

Copyright © 2011 Hanna-Barbera. SCOOBY-DOO and all related characters and elements are trademarks of and © Hanna-Barbera.

Used under license by Scholastic Inc. All rights reserved. Published by Scholastic Inc. SCHOLASTIC and associated logos are trademarks and/or registered trademarks of Scholastic Inc.

12 11 10 9 8 7 6 5 4 3 2 1   11 12 13 14 15/0

Designed by Henry Ng
Printed in the U.S.A.   40
First printing, September 2011

SCHOLASTIC INC.

New York   Toronto   London   Auckland
Sydney   Mexico City   New Delhi   Hong Kong

'Tis the night before Christmas, and Scooby and the kids from Mystery, Inc. are heading to Daphne's uncle's house in Mills Corner.

I HOPE WE GET THERE SOON. THE SNOW IS GETTING WORSE.

The Mystery Machine skids to the side of the icy road, knocking over the presents inside the van.

The gang scrambles outside to check on the Mystery Machine. That's when they hear loud screams.

JEEPERS! I WONDER WHAT THAT WAS ALL ABOUT.

CREEPY SNOWMAN! LIKE, RUN FOR YOUR LIVES!

The gang escapes from the snowman — and crash-lands in front of the town inn.

YOU'D BEST LEAVE WINTER HOLLOW. THERE'S NO CHRISTMAS HERE, THANKS TO THE SNOW MONSTER!

CRASH!

There's a loud noise from the street outside. The gang runs outside to investigate.

THE SNOW MONSTER DESTROYED MY CHIMNEY! HOW IS SANTA GOING TO COME NOW?

A little boy explains that he was waiting at home for Santa when the snow monster wrecked his chimney.

IT'S TIME TO CATCH THAT SNOWMAN. LET'S FOLLOW HIS TRACKS!

It isn't long before the gang finds what they're looking for.

ZOINKS!

RUN!

Fred, Daphne, Velma, Shaggy, and Scooby hide in an old shed.

SORRY, MAN. LIKE, OCCUPIED!

BRRR!

The snowman picks up the shed and throws it!

HMMM . . . THAT SNOW MONSTER KEEPS DESTROYING CHIMNEYS, AND THAT SURE HAS HELPED BUSINESS HERE AT THE INN.

THIS IS PROFESSOR HIGGENSON. HE WROTE A BOOK ABOUT THE SNOW MONSTER. MAYBE HE CAN HELP.

THE SNOW MONSTER IS THE GHOST OF BLACKJACK BRODY. LONG AGO, BRODY STOLE GOLD FROM SEAMUS FAGIN.

Velma reads from the professor's book.

IT SAYS HERE THAT BRODY GOT AWAY. ACCORDING TO LEGEND, HE WAS FROZEN INSIDE A SNOWMAN, AND THE STOLEN GOLD WAS NEVER FOUND.

Blackjack Brody

The gang heads outside to do a little more investigating.

THAT SNOWMAN COMES BACK EVERY CHRISTMAS TO LOOK FOR THE GOLD. HE TARGETS THE OLDEST HOUSES IN TOWN. I BET HE LOOKS IN JEB'S HOUSE NEXT!

LET'S CHECK IT OUT!

Scooby and the kids peek into Jeb's house. Guess who's coming to Christmas dinner!

JEEPERS!

The gang hides, then follows the snow monster back outside.

Fred, Daphne, and Velma throw snowballs at the snow monster, chasing it toward the ice . . .

But the snow monster's loud roar starts a deep crack across the ice.

Daphne and Velma help Scooby and Shaggy warm up.

SHERIFF! WHAT ARE YOU DOING HERE?

I WAS LOOKING FOR THE SNOW MONSTER. I FOUND SUSPICIOUS FOOTPRINTS NEAR JEB'S HOUSE.

The gang heads back to the inn to plan their next move.

I WONDER ABOUT THAT SHERIFF.

WHAT ABOUT THE INNKEEPER? HE'S GETTING RICH EVERY WINTER.

Fred pulls out the professor's book, and Daphne notices something funny about his name. . . .

WILLIAM FAGIN HIGGENSON! HE MUST BE RELATED TO THE SEAMUS FAGIN WHO LOST HIS GOLD TO BLACKJACK BRODY!

THIS BOOK SAYS BLACKJACK BRODY IS BURIED IN THE TOWN CEMETERY. SHAGGY, YOU AND SCOOBY STAY HERE AND GET WARM. GIRLS, **LET'S GO!**

As Shaggy and Scooby sit by the fireplace, an icy draft blows down the chimney. The fire goes out, and the room grows cold.

UH-OH, SCOOB. HE'S BACK!

In the dark, Shaggy and Scooby stumble into a box of Christmas lights.

The two buddies run up the stairs and out onto the rooftop. They need to find a way down, fast.

Fred has a plan to melt the snowman — the town's heat lamps!

Daphne hits a switch, and all the heat lamps turn on at once.

OH, NO! I'M MELTING!

LET'S SEE WHO'S INSIDE.

25

Velma pushes a red button on the machine.
It opens up to reveal . . .

PROFESSOR HIGGENSON!

Velma picks up a brick from the broken chimney and wipes away the soot. The brick is made of pure gold!

OKANAGAN REGIONAL LIBRARY
3 3132 03350 6926